Reds

Nicole Forbes

Copyright © 2023 by Nicole Forbes

All rights reserved.

No portion of this book may be reproduced in any form without written permission from the publisher or author, except as permitted by U.S. copyright law.

Contents

Prologue	1
1. Chapter 1	7
2. Chapter 2	15
3. Chapter 3	25
4. Chapter 4	30
5. Chapter 5	36
6. Chapter 6	42
7. Chapter 7	49
8. Chapter 8	56
9. Chapter 9	63
10. Chapter 10	69
11. Chapter 11	75
12. Chapter 12	81
13. Chapter 13	87

Prologue

It's funny how one little incident, one minor mistake, can turn your entire world around.

How one stranger, one night, leaves you in a forever bond with their actions. The actions that taint your mind every waking moment. The actions that left you to think of how they affected you every second of every day.

Left to think, if you just did that one thing differently, how would things be?

The day her life switched around was more than complicated. But she remembered it more than anything else. The day she met him.

The eyes that roamed her body, the smirk that pulled his lips, the dimples that delved into his cheeks. The fingers that twisted his rings, the small scar on his top lip that became hidden when he talked. She remembered it all.

She was eighteen. Snuck into a bar with her friends for the first time on the night of her birthday. October twenty-fifth. The night air was nippy, making her regret the dress her friend had talked her into. She even remembered the exact dress she wore. A pink satin slip dress with pink, glittery heels her friend had borrowed her. They stood outside for hours and even upon Isabella's request to go somewhere else instead of waiting in the cold, they consistently said this place was the best.

They were right of course, it was huge and had three different bars. There was even a swimming pool near the back which is why she had worn her suit underneath.

Their fake IDs had worked, not that they paid much attention, and the three of them went straight to the bar for her first drink, even though not being of age. Her friends had a history of drinking, so it was nothing new to them, but for Izzy, she was nervous. Nervous of how she would react.

She ordered something fruity, a tequila sunrise that her friend, Naomi, suggested was one of her favorites. Upon tasting it, she couldn't taste much alcohol. More orange and pomegranate. She didn't think it was affecting her much. Until she ordered another, and another, and eventually a few different drinks.

In the midsts of her state she had lost her friends, her vision loopy but she did find the dance floor. And with a drink in hand, she decided to let loose and have a little fun, dancing her heart out with all sorts of people. The biggest grin was on her face when hands wrapped around her waist and wandered her body.

"Hello there, little red," the man whispered in her ear huskily, feeling her body shudder from his deep voice. She turned, his hands following her hips that swayed to the loud music.

"Hi!" She giggled in her wasted state, taking another sip of her drink.

"You, little girl, I know you're not twenty-one," he chuckled, licking his lips and capturing her chin between his fingers. "Naughty little thing," he tsked, pulling her closer as a finger wrapped around a strand of her curly, red hair.

She pouted, "It's my birthday!" Then pushing him a little and stumbling through the crowd of pushing bodies. She began to strip her dress and shoes off, and the whole time he watched, seeing her cute little ass and smaller breasts restricted by the bathing suit she wore. She was more petite, so tiny in his eyes compared to him.

It left so many ideas in his mind.

He chuckled and followed after her as she nearly fell into the pool. Luckily no one else was in there, barely anyone was even in that section of the club besides a few drunken wanderers.

She sunk into the water, hair getting soaked and going straight momentarily until she pulled her head up and a few curls sprung up quickly. She caught his eyes as he crouched down, swimming to the man that she didn't even know.

"You're pretty," she giggled, biting her lip as she pushed herself up more to almost be right in his face. Her hands cupped his cheeks gently, and he basked in the feeling, not even caring that she would get him soaked.

She pulled him down, examining his features until suddenly pulled him into the pool with her. She laughed as he came up, hair in his face which he had to sweep back. An almost irritated smile stretched his lips as he swam over to her, trapping her against the wall which stopped her giggles.

"You really are a naughty girl, aren't you little red?" His thumb pulled down her bottom lip and watching the slight lust fill her irises as she melted into his arms.

"You want me, baby..." he chuckled, pulling her closer to him, "Don't you?" She blushed and hid her face in his chest. He leaned down into her neck, kissing gently along her shoulder, "I know I want you," he took one of her hands, guiding it below the warm water and to the imprint in his pants. She squealed, almost going to move her hand but he kept it there. And soon enough, she was feeling along the length of it and looking up at his arrogant expression.

She let out a whimper while looking up at him and he knew for a fact she had no experience. He could tell.

"Little baby...you're a virgin aren't you?" She nodded slowly with a blush imprinted into her pale skin, making it stand out more.

"Mm, I think I know the perfect little gift for you, little red," he chuckled. "Don't you think so...Izzy?" In her state she didn't even begin to question how he knew her name, just too caught up in drunken lust.

———————

His lips wandered every part of her skin, their sweaty bodies covered in a sheet as he lie on top of her. Her legs continued to shake from the pleasure she'd received and continued to receive as he thrust slowly into her.

Her body trembled below him as he took her waist in his hands. "So tiny baby...my tiny little red," she whimpered, wrapping her arms around his neck to feel him closer as he thrust slowly, hiking her legs up with his thighs. He kissed her neck needily, leaving little nips and marks along it before moving down to her chest.

He took a pink, hard nipple into his mouth, first licking over it and feeling the goosebumps that arose on her skin from her shudder. She moaned, feeling him thrust up into her hard. "S-So good," her voice cracked, squeezing her eyes closed and panting.

"Your cunt is so needy, baby," he chuckled, speeding up but gradually, wanting to draw out her pleasure agonizingly. He kissed her shoulder beside her collarbone, going up and whispering, "You want me to breed you? To fill you with my cum? You've been such a good girl baby, I think you deserve it," She moaned at the thought of him breeding her, to be filled by him.

"P-Please, please breed me," she pulled him closer so all his weight laid on her.

His strokes became long and hard until his arms wrapped around her waist and flipped them. She laid on top of him as he held her, thrusting up into her and listening to her meek little whines and whimpers. "Trust me, little red, I will," he chuckled and began thrusting faster, chasing her third orgasm of the night and his first which he could feel approaching.

He thrust his hips up and up again, over and over as his cock convulsed and suddenly shot his cum up into her. She moaned as she came all over his cock at the same time, clenching around him and milking him. He wasn't even worried about her getting pregnant, it would keep her close.

Because now, she'd never be leaving.

Chapter 1

 Two years later

"You get one phone call," They took her phone out of a little bag and dropped it into her awaiting hands.

"B-But who do I call?" The officer just shrugged and turned his back to leave the cell. She had no one to call, and didn't know any numbers that would pick up. Well, that wasn't all true. She did know one that would always answer, but there was no way she could call him. Not after the amount of effort put in just to make sure he doesn't find her.

She hadn't spoken to her parents since graduation, and all her friends had ghosted her over the years. Her siblings didn't give a damn, and it's not like any of them would have to money to bail her out.

How did this even happen?

Resisting arrest, assault on a police officer; She never did any of those things, it was all just one huge misunderstanding. Bail was set low, but still ten grand, and she only had about ten dollars on her.

She sat down on the bench, holding her head in her hands as she tried to think of someone that would answer her call while also be willing enough to pay the bail. But only one came to mind. One that would do both without a complaint, but would come with severe consequences.

It was either that or stay in here for at least three years. For something that was a mistake.

Here goes nothing.

With each press of the familiar number, she got more and more nervous, each memory being dug up after so long of burying them six feet under. Everything he did, his certain behaviors and restrictions. They all came rushing back in a pain-filled blur.

Tears welled in her eyes when she lifted the phone to her ear, hearing the agonizing ring until a woman answered. "Mr. Russo's office," She greeted.

"H-Hi um...can I speak to Xavier?"

"May I ask who this is and what it's about?" She stopped for a moment, *what the hell am I doing? Do I really wanna go down this path again?*

"I'm an old friend, I just need to speak with him,"

"And your name is?" She thought fast, blurting out the first name that came to mind.

"Benji," which was one of his close friends. She waited and waited, hearing the clicks of a keyboard in the background.

"Alright! I'm putting you through, please hold!" A loud breath of relief was let out, why she didn't know. She was about to talk to the man she hadn't in almost two years. She didn't even know if he was still looking for her. Upon moving to San Diego, she figured it was enough distance between the two that it was impossible for him to find her. All the hitchhiking, trading favors just for some cash, all this just to come right back to him.

"Perché cazzo stai chiamando da qui?" Her breath hitched upon hearing the familiar Italian accent and his angry tone. Her hands began to shake, barely able to hold the phone to her ear as a silence fell over the line. "Bene?" He asked.

She took a deep breath, a single tear rushing down her cheek "X-Xavier," Was all she could muster out.

Across the states, Xavier stood abruptly from his chair, lips parting in shock. His fist clenched at his side, eyes jotting around before turning to the large window behind him. "Where are you?" Was the first thing he asked, knowing exactly who that little nervous voice was. He heard her sniffle.

"Xavier I-I need help,"

"Where are you, little red?" He waited, his patience growing thin, very thin. He was itching to know where she'd been hiding all these years. So hidden not even his best people could find her.

"San Diego," He ground his teeth together but grabbed his coat and keys, rushing out of his office door and narrowly avoiding the people around him.

"What did you do?" He asked sternly; when approaching his secretary's desk, he quickly told her to cancel everything for today and get him a flight to San Diego, ignoring her protests and listening to the meek girl on the other line.

"I-I got arrested, they accused me of something that was a misunderstanding,"

"What's the bail?" He immediately asked.

"Ten thousand," She said nervously, playing with the ends of her hair while looking around the empty cell, and at the officers looking at her like a piece of meat.

"Hurry up in there, Williams!" He suddenly yelled upon seeing her stare; she jumped, the shaking in her hands worsening.

"I-I have to go,"

"Don't you fucking hang up on me Isabella-" But she did, finally taking in a deep breath that she seemed to be held during the entire call. Hearing his voice was traumatizing enough.

She set the phone beside her, rubbing her face and trying to control her rapid breaths. He'll be here by tomorrow. It was impossible for her to even begin to prepare herself for seeing him again. He was probably going to be seething, and who knows what he was to do.

A sleepless night in an uncomfortable bunk was all Isabella received that night. Her thoughts ran rapid, scenarios playing over and over of what could happen.

They moved her into a different cell, one with another woman who hadn't said a word to her, just slept continuously on her top bunk. They had also stuck her in an orange jumpsuit which was more than uncomfortable. Her morning was embarrassing, no privacy whatsoever to do anything. When everyone had to go down for breakfast, the officers were teasing and rude, seeming to want to pick on her the most.

A few men in specific seemed to eye her up and down and tried to get a little close, but luckily she escaped in time. She recognized one of those men to be the one she supposedly assaulted.

The food was pretty plain, all she had was an apple as nothing else seemed appealing. A lot of the women in here seemed to be decently comfortable with each other, so she decided to sit at an empty table to not cause any trouble. Those TV shows she used to watch about inmates getting in each other's faces scared her too much to do otherwise.

After, they were all directed to go to the showers, where there weren't curtains but instead tiny walls between each one. A woman officer stood in there but didn't seem to look at anyone, just made sure no one was getting in any trouble.

While all the women were stripping with no issue, Isabella backed herself into a corner and slowly did so, paranoid and looking around constantly but no one seemed to care thankfully. They were all chattering away.

She went to one of the showers, pulling it to turn on and gasping as the cold spits of water hit her in a rush. She did everything she could to cover herself while trying to adjust, but the temperature wouldn't change. So to get it done and over with, she quickly lathered her hair in the shampoo provided and washed her body.

Her curls sprung up quickly after the shower, coming down almost to her waist thickly.

The officers forced them all to head back to their cells, and with her only being in a towel she rushed to not run into those officers again, but fate wasn't on her side in any way these past few years.

"Running somewhere?" One teased and cornered her, another popping in behind her.

"I-I need to get dressed so..." She trailed off, clutching her towel like her life depended on it and keeping her head down. "P-Please let me through," She tried to squeeze her way through but was only pushed back. It wasn't till a woman officer came over and pushed them away, yelling at her to get to her cell, was she able to escape before anything else were to happen.

Her cellmate was already in there, not giving a care about not being dressed and only giving a subtle glance towards Isabella who rushed to get the clean clothes on her bunk. She went to the side of the bunks, dropping her towel and quickly putting on the fresh underwear and jumpsuit.

Her red curls fell, and she tried to maintain them but there was no use. She left them be and went to her bunk.

―――――――――

"Williams," An officer came into their cell, looking straight at Isabella. "C'mon, you're out,"

"What?"

"Someone made your bail, let's go," A chill shot down her spine, he's here.

She followed the woman out and down the hallway of other cells to a heavily guarded door. Thankfully she didn't see any of the police officers that had been giving her a hard time. It was straight, peaceful. The last bit of peace she'd have in a while.

Inside there were police everywhere, so far no sign of him but the woman led her to a desk. "Name?"

"Isabella Willams," The woman handed over a bag of her clothes with a sticky note on them. "The man over there took your phone. Go to the check-out corner and sign," The woman said with a monotonous voice, one that was just rushing her to get away so she could go back to her phone.

Isabella looked to where the woman gestured to, seeing the man behind it all standing with his hands in his pockets.

Xavier was looking directly at her, a grin stretching onto his face at the sight of her.

Chapter 2

Her body trembled at the sight of the man - taking in the difference versus two years ago. His dark hair was longer, curling slightly at the ends but his stubble was well taken care of and still the same. His blue eyes shone with a darkness that didn't help her shakes.

She looked down, gripping her bag of clothes to her chest and walking over to the next counter. A man slid her a clipboard and pen, which she went to pick up when a hand snaked around her waist.

His head nuzzled against the side of her head as he whispered, "I'll lock you away and throw away the fucking key if you ever do something like that again," The officer glanced at then suspiciously, watching her hand shakily signing the paper quickly and nearly tossing it back to him.

"Go change over there and leave your uniform in the bucket," He instructed and Isabella took that time to escape from Xavier's arms and rush into the changing room. Although his threat lived vividly in her mind, this was the last tiny bit of freedom she'd get in who knows how long. She didn't know how things will go this time around.

She quickly changed back into her outfit, which at the time was a loose-fitted dress that dropped about mid-thigh. Now looking at it, if she knew she'd be in this position right now, she would've never worn it seeing how Xavier would use it to his advantage. Maybe he's different.

Although that was very unlikely with the words just whispered into her ear. Lock me up..? He...wouldn't, right?

Not again.

She exited the room to see Xavier waiting close by, keeping his eyes still on her and the hesitation when she walked over to him. But when she took too long, Xavier grabbed her hand and tugged her along, getting multiple looks from fellow officers. Especially one she was rather familiar with who focused a little too long on her legs.

He didn't say a word to her the whole time he was dragging her through the parking lot - which in all honesty was scarier than him yelling at her.

He shoved her against his car, pouncing on her and trapping her. The fear in her eyes was exhilarating to him, feeling her body tremble in fear as he rose his hands to cup her face. The involuntary flinch that followed, squeezing her precious little gem eyes closed but then relaxing as he just held her. "You're lucky I'm so merciful baby...but only for now." He dug his head into the soft red locks of her hair, twisting a curl around his finger and smiling at the familiar smell of honey that laced her pale skin. The red blemishes on her shoulders and elbows were always something so beautiful to him, but for a reason, he didn't know.

A tear dropped from her eye, sliding down her cheek. "Why are you crying doll? Aren't you happy to see me?" He whispered softly into her ear, feeling the shudder and seeing the bumps arise in her skin.

"I-I'm sorry," was all she could mutter, her little green gem eyes flickering all over the place except his own.

"Are you, Izzy?" He chuckled, gently stroking her cheek. "Two fucking years. Two; I looked night and day for you but it was like you vanished into thin air." His other hand went up and stroked down her hair. "I will say it's impressive how well you got by without any of my men pinpointing you," A kiss laid on her cheek, "but that's not the point."

He pulled back from her neck, staring down at the deep green eyes that patterned her iris beautifully. They were glossy, shining with the tears he had created but he just wiped them all away.

He leaned in, their heartbeats syncing together with Isabella's a little more aggressive. Her lips parted involuntarily, tiny gasps for breaths all to be heard as his lips grazed hers. He groaned, taking her cheeks aggressively into his hands and forcing their lips together. All he could hear was her meek little whimpers that were soon to be drowned out.

"Shush, baby," He said swiftly before their lips were back on each other, his body forcing his on hers, nearly suffocating her between him and the car.

His tongue swept against her lip, smiling at her lack of breath as she tried to keep up with him.

"X-Xavier-" She meekly let out when he finally let her go but not far as his arms around her waist were tight.

"You, little red," His eyes pierced down into hers as he panted slightly, "You're not going out of my sight." His thumb brushed against her kiss-swollen lips.

The door beeped a few times as he slid the card out from it and the door popped open. A gentle hand pushed her into the hotel room and she admired it for a moment. The room had a separate kitchen and one queen-sized bed. A large TV hung up on the wall across from it and there was a sliding glass door with a clear view of the beach.

He set her bag in a chair with some of his stuff and watched as she hesitantly sat on the end of the bed and looked up at him with her big doe eyes. She gulped, gripping the duvet as he approached her and swept her curls off her shoulder.

"I've missed you so much Izzy," Her lip wobbled slightly.

"I'm sorry...please don't hurt me," She muttered, closing her eyes as his hand stroked against her cheek.

He hummed, "You know I never would," He sat down next to her, taking her cheek and turning it toward himself. "Just like you know you've missed me, no matter how much you tell yourself you didn't."

Their lips brushed gently together, her eyes nearly fluttering shut as his thumb swept over her cheek in the softest of touches. "Didn't you, Kitten?" His lips pressed against the corner of her lips before molding onto hers, smirking as she kissed him back more eagerly.

Two years without being touched, loved, and then suddenly receiving more attention from the man who had given it to her for years had gotten to her.

Their relationship was complicated. It always had been but she stuck because all in all, she loved him. But some of his tendencies scared the daylights out of her.

He pulled her onto his lap, hands roaming her frail body. "Let me have you, baby, I'll give you everything you've been craving and more," He whispered huskily only to hear her whimper. But he could feel the heat between her legs as she tried to hide her face in his neck.

"You missed me, baby, it's okay to admit it. You ran but you came back like a good girl..." His fingers fiddled with the zipper on her dress, slowly pulling it down. "Let me reward you. All you have to do is relax and let me do all the work for you, do you want that?" Her dress slid off her body while he twisted them to lay down on the bed. He moved between her legs, pressing his growing erection into her and smiling at the little mewl she let out. She covered her face in embarrassment, the color of her face changing from the pale he always knew to bright pink.

"Y-Yes," She gave in, peeking between her fingers and watching his grin grow bigger.

"Good girl," he leaned down and whispered into her ear. Her heart pounded away as his fingers worked in her bra, slipping it down her arms and then going down to her thin panties.

She hesitantly reached up towards his chest, running her hands down his exposed collarbone and beginning to undo his buttons. He groaned at her touch, her soft, cold hands reminding him of every time they've been together.

He helped her take off his shirt swiftly, loving the way her eyes roamed his chiseled chest and the markings of ink that laid upon it.

His hand held hers gently, lifting it and kissing every little finger of hers and then up her arm till her neck which he littered with soft kisses. His teeth began to leave their mark on every place they could touch. Her neck, shoulder, collarbone and soon reached down to her breast.

The whole time he thrust his hips into her so he made sure she felt what she was doing to him. He could feel the moisture of herself leaking onto his pants even as she tried to hide it by closing her legs but she couldn't.

His hand trailed down her stomach as he kissed and nipped at her nipple, slowly and surely until reaching the soft skin between her legs. He grazed her clit which left a mewl to spill from her lips.

"So pretty and pink," he hummed, gazing among her wet little pussy as he spread her lips. She shuddered as he blew along her clit that throbbed to be touched. "My baby is so touched starved isn't she... tell me Izzy, has any other man dared to touch what's mine?"

She didn't have the guts to answer. Living on the streets was hard, and you had to do what you had to do to make it.

"Isabella," He gripped her cheeks roughly. "Did someone touch this little cunt of yours? Don't lie to me baby it'll only make it worse." Her lip trembled as she slowly nodded, not daring to look him in the eyes that were seething.

"How many?" His thumb rolled her clit around which had her arching her back. Again, she didn't answer so he tapped her cheek.

"O-One..." She shakily answered, her body buzzing with nerves.

He hummed, sinking two fingers into her soaked cunt slowly. "Tell me, baby," He looked down to her leaking pussy, smiling at how well she took his two fingers, thrusting into her and curling upwards. He let her cheek go, going down to his belt and quickly unbuckling it and taking out his cock.

"Was he as big as me? Bigger?" His nine inches laid against her cunt, and her face exploded as she felt it against her. "Did he know how to pleasure you? Were you able to cum as you could so easily with me?" His head rubbed against her clit as his fingers sped up in her.

"Answer me!" He exclaimed suddenly and made her jump.

"No...h-he couldn't do any of those things," He smiled, directing his head down to her entrance and slowly edging in.

"He couldn't fill you, could he baby?" She shook her head in complete embarrassment. "Couldn't breed you as I can. That's why you don't go to other men to please this little cunt. Only I can. No other man will ever be able to satisfy you. And you know that,"

Her moans finally spilled out as he suddenly thrust deep inside her but not too deep to not hit her cervix. "W-Wait - I'm not on the pill-" He just chuckled and continued to thrust into her.

"That's too bad baby, maybe if I get you knocked up you'll learn to never leave me." Her mind was too clouded with pleasure to even try to stop him. In fact, it was the opposite. She wrapped her legs around him as she throbbed under his touch, gripping the sheets so hard her knuckles turned white as her back arched at the pleasure she received.

"Look at that," he chuckled, "Already cumming all over my dick. He couldn't make you cum that quick could he?" She shook her head as she met his thrust, riding out her high before collapsing but of course, he didn't stop. Instead, he flipped her over and pressed her face into the pillow.

Tears fell down her cheeks at such an immense feeling that filled her, biting into the pillow to hide her screams as he hit every perfect spot. Their lewd noises filled the room, the sound of slapping, whimpers, and moans.

"Your pussy is mine Izzy, no man touches what's mine. I'll fucking kill him. If anyone touches you," He leaned over her body, gripping her hair and yanking her head up as he whispered in her ear, "I'll fucking kill them."

His hand snaked around her body and found her clit again which just made her more of a moaning mess. His tongue licked up her shoulder to her neck where he kissed and nipped aggressively. He felt her cunt clench around him.

"Gonna cum again, little red? Go ahead baby, cum as much as you want." She screamed and moaned his name as she came once more, not being able to take the sensitivity that followed as he continued to thrust in her.

He continued for hours on end, dragging her into every position imaginable until they ended with her in his lap as she bounced on him, his hands on her hips to guide as he watched her lustfully. He took in the pleasure that filled her face, her parted lips, tear-filled eyes, and cheeks that were as red as cherries.

"X-Xavier I can't," She cried as he urged her to cum one final time.

"Yes you can baby, c'mon, just one more time love and you're done," He groaned, feeling his own release edging up.

"I can't." She cried again, hugging herself to him as he took over thrusting into her. Her body shook in pleasure when his fingers rolled and stroked along her clit, feeling herself clench around him as her body rolled into yet another orgasm.

"There you go, good girl," He praised as he felt her cum spread down his raging cock that began to throb. He held her as tight as possible before thrusting deep into her and releasing, breeding her to the max. She moaned loudly at the feeling, her legs shaking against him before her body finally gave out and she sobbed into his neck. He continued to coo and praise her for her amazing job over the hours of endless pleasure.

Chapter 3

Xavier stroked gently along her arm as she drifted in and out of sleep, her body still aching and shaking. Whether that be from pain mixed pleasure or her growing fear for him.

"I've missed you so much Izzy," He laid a kiss on her bruised shoulder, her eyes squeezing closed. She wasn't even able to process all of this. How she had given into him so easy like always.

His arms curled around her to bring her closer, laying delicate kiss after kiss on her back, hands wandering down her waist. Her eyes stayed on the wall in front of her, eyes dry from crying so much. She stared blankly, letting him do as he pleased for the time being as her body was too tired to protest anymore.

"You'll never leave me again baby, I know you won't." His hands gripped at her waist a bit too harsh and had her letting out a small whine. He began to lay kisses down her back while holding her close so she couldn't get away.

She hesitantly cuddled into the arm that held her so tightly, drifting off to sleep as best as she could until she woke up at the peeks of dawn.

He was gone out of bed as she sat up, observing the small room around her and seeing no trace of him as if it all had been a dream. But the soreness told her otherwise.

She covered herself at the sound of the door beeping, bringing the thin sheet up to her neck to cover her nudeness.

He stepped in, eyes directly on her while doing so and taking in her nervous form.

"How did you sleep, baby?" He asked calmly, walking over to the bed and sitting beside her. His hand reached up and twisted around a curl, watching her visible flinch before hesitantly going back.

"U-um...good," she spoke softly, looking away from his direction and hearing him tsk. "Y-You came in me-" Her eyes widened as she remembered. But instead of freaking out like her, he merely chuckled at her panicked state.

"I had a vasectomy a year or so ago. You're not going to get pregnant baby," she let out a relieved sigh, her whole body untensing

"We're going home today," he said, making her tense back up at the words. She had to repeat them in her head just to fully grasp what he had said. His eyes watched as hers darted every which way, as she clenched the bed sheets at the sound of home.

"I-I don't want to go back there," She whispered meekly, head bowing and looking to the left.

"Why not baby?" His teeth nearly gritted, "All your friends are there, your parents, our home." His finger nudged her chin up to see her tear-filled eyes.

"Please...please just let me go," She damn near sobbed as she was forced to look up at him.

Her wrists were scooped up and pulling her onto his lap where he grabbed her jaw to force her to look him in the eyes. "Look at me, little red," he held her wrists tightly.

"I am not letting you go. Two years Izzy, two fucking years I searched high and low. And may God be damned if he thinks I'm going to let you go ever again." He brought his head close and upon whispering those last words, his lips sunk onto hers, taking them in a fiery passion that made her head spin in such a way. His hand dug into the back of her head, pushing her to him where his lips moved slowly but passionately.

"You're mine, Izzy,"

———————————

The house, the home she thought she'd never see again now stood tall in front of her.

The gates slowly opened upon their arrival, the black gates parting as the car rolled in slowly to the large house before them. Their home.

The home that had been there for a little over three years. The car pulled to the front before finally coming to a stop. Xavier stepped out of the car before she could, stepping over to her side while she gathered her bags, and opening her door for her.

One of the maids rushed over and took all the things she tried to carry from her, scurrying back into the open door.

Xavier took her hand gently and brought her out of the car.

The night sky surrounded them, stars glistening above the two as they stared at each other for a moment, of course, Isabella breaking their eye contact.

She looked up at the house, remembering the last time she was there. It wasn't easy getting out, and she knew, knowing him, it would be impossible now.

She remembered the fresh air of freedom upon crawling out that door and for once being able to get by safely without being caught by him.

The time she was caught by him…

She shuddered at the memory and gulped hard, looking up at the man who guided her in by a hand on her back but he never looked back at her.

The maids had propped open the door, guards waiting for them as they stepped in and she took in everything with a deep, trembling breath. Everything looked exactly the same as if she had never left.

It was kept tidy and organized, thanks to the maids but Xavier also hated things being a mess. A pet peeve of his.

"How about a bath?" He wrapped his arm around her and whispered. His head buried in her hair, twisting a red curl around his finger and smiling. She didn't dare say no.

He took her hand and led her to the spiral scare case behind the living room that led up to a long hallway going both ways. He took her to the left with maids shuffling after to take their things to their room which is exactly where they were headed.

After the maids dropped their things off, they hurried out to give the couple room. Isabella sat down on the end of the bed to take her shoes off as her feet ached, but Xavier did it for her just in time as she began to. He slid her black heels off, seeing the imprints of the shoe along her feet, and gently rubbed them.

A blush dusted along her pale cheeks as he looked up at her with such a look that had her insides twisting.

He first kissed her shin, lifting her leg and then kissing her knee until he moved between the two legs. He spread them slowly, all the while looking up at her as he hiked her dress up he went so close, all the way to her inner thigh where his nose brushed her core and sent chills down her body, but he stopped and sat up.

"Let's go take that bath."

Chapter 4

The bath was warm, little white flowers floating within the foggy water from the bath bomb. Everything he knew she loved.

She stood in front of the tub, looking over the rosy water as Xavier stepped up to her. He slid her hair onto her shoulder, holding her by her hips and kissing the back of her neck. A rush of chills and goosebumps sent through her body at the soft touch.

His finger tips slid up the back of her arm and to her shoulder where he pulled the straps on her mini sun dress down, watching as it pooled at her feet and she stepped out of it.

He turned her, looking over the nervous look as he brought her hands to his shirt. She understood what he was gesturing to, beginning to undo the buttons of his dress shirt until he finally just shrugged it off. As they stood in front of each other, half dressed, Xavier couldn't helo but take her soft, plump lips again, tasting the strawberry of her lip balm.

He groaned from the softness of her lips, feeling them caress his own and he smiled. He knew no matter how much she hid it, she loved him. She always will. He gave her everything she ever wanted, and it weighed out the cons.

Her body had ached for that same attention he gave her all those years when she had left. She hated it, but she did. Not that she'll ever admit it.

He undressed the both of them, picking her up and setting her into the bath and she shuddered at the warm water. Her body sunk into the water, her hair up to the middle getting soaked as she scooped her hands in the water and gathered a few flowers. All the while, Xavier was slipping in behind her, holding her tight against him.

He ran his finger tips gentky along her back as she was leaned over. He gathered water in his palm and poured it down her back before leaning over as well a laying a soft kiss.

"I could get you your old job back if you'd like, not that you need it. Get you back into classes, anything you want Izzy," He pulled her tighter so she leaned back more, kissing the crease of her shoulder. "How does that sound, hm?" She fiddled with the petals in the water, tearing them from the flowers in her anxious state.

"T-That sounds good," she said meekly.

"Of course you'll have someone at your side the whole time. I know how you are. You're an opportunist." He raked her hair back, "I like it in a way..." he chuckled, "It gives me opportunities to play with you," her nose burned at the feeling of wanting to cry, lip wobbling at the feeling of his lips planting kiss after kiss until he took a loofah and began to lather her body.

"But you've been such a good girl here recently," His breath followed her skin up her neck and jaw. "Baby, do you remember our first time?" he captured her ear lobe between his teeth momentarily, "In that pool...everyone watched as you lost your virginity," She whimpered at the humiliating memory, tainted with drunken lust. She never wanted to look back on that day, it was too embarrassing, and the change of her life.

"You were so embarrassed when your friends came to find you," he laughed, running the loofah down her shoulder and arm. "I knew I would have so much fun with you,"

He chuckled, "Just like that time..." he turned her around, sitting her on his lap and looking up at her, "I whipped you in front of everyone,"

"Y-You're insane," she slowly and hesitantly wrapped her arms around his neck, but in the midsts of doing so, he whispered,

"But you love it,"

Her eyes gazed at all of her old clothes, folded so perfect and neat, just exactly how she had left them. Xavier knew she would get her back, so he never moved a thing. But he never slept in that bed.

He refused to, it was theirs. And only theirs. Both. Not one. He slept in his other homes, vowing to not go back to that one until he finds her. It had been just as long for him since being in this house as it had for her.

"I'll work on getting you back into the university tomorrow, for your job its the same. Although I don't know why you'd want to work there, paid so low when I can give you plenty," he tsked, turning to her as she slid on a satin night gown.

"It's not about the money, T-The older woman, Betty, she just needs some help,"

She climbed up into bed with him, slipping under the covers and glancing at his conouter, seeing a bunch of things she didn't care to understand. She glanced yp to his face, seeing hin focused and she hesitantly scooted closer, wrapping a shakey hand around his bicep and leaning her head on it as well.

He looked down at her mess of red curls, stopping for a moment. He observed her for a moment, wondering what she may be up to when he just leaned down and kissed the top of her head. "Go to bed, Izzy."

_____

"Isabella," she stopped as she came out of the bathroom, freezing at the sound of him saying her full name. "Get dressed," she nodded, scurrying over and into the closet filled with all her clothes. Of course she went with something simple and casual, not knowing where the two were going. So it was just jeans and a shirt with a flannel.

She slipped out the door where he and a guard were waiting. "Izzy, this is Antonio, he'll be going with you wherever you go," She gave the man a tight-lipped smile which he didn't bother to return, seemingly irritated with his boss's request of, in Antonio's perspective, "babysitting duty". He had better things to worry about and do than follow a little brat around all day.

"We're going ti the café now, to get you your job," Xavier spoke, looking down at the redhead who twisted a curl of her own around the tip of her finger.

"Okay," was all she said, taking the hand that he held out and leading the two down the hallway and declining down the spiral steps.

As they rolled up to the small, corner café, a flood of nostalgia hit her in a rush and she slowly smiled. Xavier led her in, where she smelled the fresh baked goodies feel the shop, the view of cinnamon rolls, brownies, cookies, everything all made her mouth water at such a delicious sight.

But the man behind the counter distracted her from all of it and she froze.

Brandon. Her old guy best friend before she left. He walked behind the counter and she noticed the limp, feeling the familiar guilt pull at her heart. Xavier went with someone towards the back, not even noticing for the time being that she wasn't there to follow, instead she stepped up towards the counter, making Brandon turn her way.

His eyes widened to the size of golf balls, tsking a step back from the counter. "I-Izzy," he stuttered, trying to process the fact that it indeed was the red head girl in front of him.

"Brandon...I-" He held up his hand, shaking his head.

"Don't," he suddenly said sternly, "Don't talk to me. Especially while that man is here,"

"B-But, please, I just wanted to say-" A hand wrapped around her arm and yanked her back, her green eyes looking up into eyes of fury, before he dragged her out.

Chapter 5

"I think I've told you before, little red," he threw her to the ground of their bedroom, slamming the door behind them and shrugging off his coat, "that you are not to talk to that boy." She backed up until her back hit the bed, lip wobbling as she looked up at him in his weirdly calm state. But she could feel the anger; radiating off him in waves.

"I-I was just-" she whimpered as his hand grabbed a hold of her jaw in a painful grip, digging his fingertips onto her cheeks.

"Did you not learn your lesson last time? When I showed you what would happen if you talked to him? As I made you watch what I was capable of?" He slowly unbuttoned his shirt and she noticed the growing bulge in her pants. "Was that not good enough for you, Izzy, hm?"

She didn't say anything, just breathed heavy as he held her tightly.

"Fucking answer me, Isabella!" He suddenly yelled and she jumped back, eyes squeezing closed as tears dripped down her cheeks.

"I-I'm sorry," She whispered so quietly, so shakily she didn't even know if he could hear her. But she didn't have time to repeat herself either, as his lips forced onto hers as he pressed her up against the bed and dragging his hands through her hair. She whimpered in the kiss, grabbing hold on his unbuttoned shirt to try and keep herself steady with his growing need.

He pushed her down till her back hit the floor, eyebrows furrowing and her hands laying gently on his chest. Despite her gentle antics, he was rough, pulling her clothes from her and feeling up her body faster than she could comprehend.

From the feeling of his lips touching her abdomen, she gasped and arched her back, feeling him travel lower until her pelvis.

He kissed her hip bone, deadly eyes looking up at her and not liking the sight of her closed eyes.

He slapped her thigh, getting her attention right as he devoured her. Tongue delving through her swollen lips as feeling her thighs clench around his head and her beautiful whisper of moans. Her body writhed from even the simple pleasure.

Her nails scraped gently through his scalp, clenching the dark strands of his hair and gasping for air.

He sat up, lips and stubble wet before unbuckling his belt and dragging her by her thighs up to him, laying her thighs over his own and thrusting into her.

"Ah!" She yelped, digging her nails into his skin at the sudden pressure of him filling her, damn near balls deep.

He watched her with lust filled eyes and parted lips, hooking his arms around her thighs and using them to thrust into her, watching as her little breasts bounced with every move.

She knew by now to keep her eyes open, looking up with her own lust-filled eyes and watching his every move to know what to expect.

But no matter what she did, ahe would never understand his next moves; know what he was thinking. He was impossible to read.

Nothing but the sounds of him fucking her could be heard, he was too pissed to say anything to her, saying everything he needed to with how rough he was on her, letting her know the intensity of his anger.

He flipped her, pushing her head into the floor by her hair and fucking her faster, hearing her stuttered moans and whines. She clawed at the ground, feeling the pleasure up in her gut and not being able to contain herself as she came all on his cock and let her body collapse.

He panted, pulling out of her and dragging her up by her hair, "C'mere," he demanded, pulling her up onky to force her back down until her lips touched the tip of his cock. She looked up at him, seeing the anger that still circled his iris in a darker tone and began to bring his cock into her mouth.

But he pulled her by her hair, "Nuh-uh," He tsked, guiding her by her hair to only lick his tip. He groaned, looking down and watching as she worked her tongue around the head expertly.

She dipped her tongue into the slit, then swirled it around to the under side until finally he let loose of his grip slightly for her to sink more into his cock.

All the while he reached between them, feeling through her wet folds and hearing a little whimper in doing so. Her smirked at her dripping self, "As much as you tell yourself you don't love me," he brought his fingers to his lips, tasting her essences and moaning at doing so. "You have a funny way of showing it, love."

———————————

Her body ached; every time they were to do any type of activity, it lasted for hours on end. His stamina was insane, and he didn't give out easy. Unlike her.

At the end of the night she could barely move, her legs too wobbly to do so but in his graciousness he carried her into the bathroom and cleaned her up. Her red curls a mess, he put up into two braids and then got her to bed.

Now, laying up , eyes opening and closung and staring at the sight of the white ceiling with strands of the suns rays warming her side, she couldn't help but think over everything.

She was so indecisive about him; he was right. She would always eventually come crawling back. He seemed to be her onky support. Even being on her own, it took restraint to not pick up the phone and call him. And even the nught before her arrest she planned to do so. It was completely impossible to escape him — he had her trapped.

The bedsheets were empty that morning, besides her body wrapped in them, Xavier was once more no where in sight.

The room had been cleaned of their destruction — Xavier had shown her whose she is. His jealousy was ravaging, destructive. He hated the sight of a man even looking at her, no matter who it may be. He knew the thoughts of men, and his beautiful little darling was one of mens taste. Small, not able to fend others off so it would be easy for anyone to snatch her up. Its why he kept her so close and locked in constantly.

With Brandon — he knew he wanted her.

The door creaked open, him being careful if she wasn't awake yet which she wasn't. Her sleep had captured her again.

A small, black box laid in his hand which he set down on the nightstand and slowly sat on the edge of the bed, sweeping loose strands away from her face and using his knuckle to stroke her cheeks, for once not flushed and instead her body laid calm and rested.

He laid his kiss on her plump and pink ones, holding the side of her face as, in her light sleep, her eyes fluttered open.

He looked down at her and gave her a small smile, then kissed her forehead.

"I'm sorry, baby," He took the box, gently laying it in her hands. "I know I was too rough on you...you're so fragile," he played with a strand of her hair, looking over her beautiful features. "I'm fucked up, I know," he leaned his forehead on hers, opening the box for her to reveal a diamond necklace,

"But I swear I'm trying."

Chapter 6

She stared into her reflection as he placed the necklace around her neck. She reached up, touching the sparkling diamond and the small chain connected to it. The pear pendant was absolutely dazzling, and gorgeous. He had amazing taste, she knew he did. He always did. From clothes to jewelry.

"Thank you," She muttered as he latched it, turning her around and stealing her lips briefly.

"I figured I would take you shopping for the day, to make up for my jealously. I'll buy you anything and everything you want," His knuckle grazed her cheek, watching happily as she leaned into the touch.

"You've already done too much...I'm really okay-"

"It's not a choice little red," she stared up at him, but just nodded and decided not to waste her breath with a protest. It's not like it would be so bad.

"Go get dressed, Izzy," he nudged her softly out of the bathroom, following her as she went to the drawers in their closet, searching through the clothes to decide what to wear.

He watched her closely, sitting on the edge of the bed and having a clear view of herself inside the closet. There was a full-length mirror inside, and he could see her little worried expression in finding what to wear until finally reached up on her tiptoes and grabbed a small dress off the hanger.

Their eyes met in the mirror, and she shied away, going to a corner of the closet where he couldn't see as well and changing out of her shirt.

He shook his head and pulled a pack of cigarettes out of his pocket and headed over to the double glass doors covered by the curtains. He pulled them back, opening up the doors and feeling the cool wind hit him and rush to fill the room and fight the heat.

He pulled out a cig, popping it into his mouth and not hesitating to light it. The warm drag traveled down the back of his throat as he inhaled, then let the smoke fall out his lips in waves. He was agitated. Maybe it was taking her out, he didn't know if she would try something.

"Xavier," Her voice followed through the large room softly, until his ears picked up on the sound and he turned to see her in a small dress, her hair done in braids and flats on her feet. She was slipping on a sweater as he took another drag from his cigarette and put it out in the tray beside him.

He turned out the balcony, exhaling his drag along the way and shutting the double doors where a few wisps of smoke traveled inside with him and wrapped around him, before finally dissipating.

"Ready?" He asked, petting over her lumps of curls and watching as she hesitantly leaned into it. She nodded.

"Listen to me very closely, little girl," he took her by her jaw painfully, and sat her down on the edge of the bed while her scared eyes fought to look up at him. "You stay by me, you are never to leave my sight, or there will be severe consequences, you hear me?"

"Y-Yes," She whispered under her breath, looking up into his eyes, knowing he would get mad if done otherwise.

He's always so angry, she thought, but in a way, he had a right to be so after what she did.

"Good," he stood her up, and the two exited their home and went on their way.

―――――――――――

Of course, when the two ventured to the mall, three other men followed suit.

He kept a grip on her hand as the two walked in, seeing the numerous people and she cowered away at the numerous looks given. Understandably so, with the three men dressed in professional attire and following with a cold look.

"Keep up, little red," he pulled her when she began to fall behind, slipping off his sunglasses and hooking them on his shirt.

They ventured around a part of the mall, him trying to get her to choose a store but instead, she would just say "Wherever you would like to go," in that little quiet voice of hers. He finally huffed in frustration, dragging her into a nearby clothing store and letting go of his death grip on her hand.

"Go. Get what you want." He sighed, rubbing a hand over his face at the sight of her very hesitantly stepping in without him being right on her.

She blinked a few times, looking around with racing thoughts, impulsive thoughts, all telling her that this was her time to finally make her move. But she wasn't that stupid.

She pulled her sweater closer to her, walking towards a rack of clothes while her flats slipped off her heels from being too big.

He watched her closely, following a few feet behind while his security team stayed at the exits just in case, all keeping their eyes on her as well. She'd been a flight risk in the past.

She walked on her tiptoes, fingers grazing over the clothes and picking out a few she liked before finally turning to Xavier and holding them out to him with no words. He cocked an eyebrow but took them, gesturing to the register and she quickly followed.

After paying they were onto the next store, shopping around until she finally got comfortable enough to be in there longer than five minutes, knowing he has all the money in the world to buy her anything. The diamond around her neck spoke to that.

It was going okay, they would chit-chat about certain clothes and certain ones he would disapprove of.

Until finally, he received a phone call.

"This better be good," he snapped at the other person on the other line, talking about a disaster at work and how he needed to come in and help fix it out.

With a roll of his eyes, he hung up the phone and instead dialed another.

Idiots, I swear. He thought, grumbling the whole way looking for her contact until finally stumbling upon it.

All the while, a few rows down, Isabella was looking at him with a curious look, a bit of fear striking her at his angry written face.

He gestured her over and she didn't waste time following his command, walking up till right in front of him and peering up at him with her big, doe eyes.

"Vieni qui al centro commerciale. Adesso." He spoke quickly before hanging up the phone and shoving it back into his pocket.

"Little red," he brushed her bangs away from her eyes. "I have to go, but I told you I would let you shop today so I'm having someone come down for you."

"S-So...you're leaving me with someone I don't even know," a little smirk caressed his lips and a low, dark, and menacing chuckle left them as he leaned back and kneeled down at her level. He saw the brightening of her eyes, the ray of hope and all he wanted to do was crush it.

In an instant, his hand was wrapped around her jaw and yanking her close till his lips grazed her ear. She let out a little whimper, holding onto his shirt to steady herself.

"Try something, little red," He whispered, "I fucking dare you," His smile grazed her cheek as that lingering look of darkness lurked around the depths of his eyes.

She stared at them, in them, her own wide and filled to the brim of sweet fear.

He stood up straight caressing her jaw and then her chin, stepping into the doorway of the shop, stepping aside.

"Wanna run, Izzy? Hm? Go ahead." That sick, darkening smile of his returned as he held his hand out, gesturing her to go. But she wasn't stupid.

She just gulped and took a step back, looking away. "I-I'm not running." She muttered weakly.

"Good girl."

Chapter 7

"Good girl," he muttered, walking back over to her shaking self and pulling her into his arms, kissing the top of her head.

"You've been such a good girl for me, Izzy," He smiled, stroking her head and glancing over to the shop workers who stared with pure shock but with one glare they were scurrying back to their jobs.

She just held herself in his arms, tears brimming her eyes but she tried to maintain herself. But she couldn't help herself. She tried to hide as tears dripped down her cheeks but he noticed by the slight shake of her body.

"C'mere baby," he tugged her away from the crowd of people in the store - knowing how easily she gets embarrassed especially as she covered her reddening face with her hands as he guided her.

He moved her into one of the dressing rooms, not caring about the protest of the woman in front of them, and sat her down on the bench.

"I'm sorry baby, I didn't mean to scare you. I know you've been very good for me," he pushed her bangs back, moving her hands away and wiping the tears that filled her face as she hiccupped. "You have since I got you back," he rubbed gently down her back and sighed.

"Here, Izzy, buy whatever you want my baby, don't worry about money."

"Y-You can't," she sniffled, balling her hands into fists, "You can't just think money fixes everything. It doesn't." She said, speaking up a little louder and turning to look him in the eyes.

"Money can't fix your abuse!" She finally exclaimed, watching the slight shock cross his face as she had never yelled at him, always too terrified to do so.

He didn't say anything, just stared at her blankly for a moment before standing up and walking out of the room to which she hesitantly followed.

A few steps beside the door, a woman stood with brown hair pulled to a ponytail. Freckles littered her face, so visible Isabella could see them across the store.

She followed after Xavier who walked scarily calm, not an emotion to be read on his chiseled features.

"This is Cassie. You are to stay by her." He handed her his card and said nothing more. Only looked down at her with a look she couldn't bear to understand, before walking off with his hands in his pockets.

Even Cassie was confused, never seeing such a way of interacting from him. So calm, as if he had the world going for him.

Izzy looked blown away, watching him walk away till he disappeared completely and even then she just stared.

Stared with a feeling creeping down on her for what awaited her later.

Oh god...what have I done? She thought.

_____

"So..." Cassie started awkwardly, looking down at the girl who held not an emotion on her face. Izzy's mind was reeling with what was to come when she returned home, what type of devilish thing he held for her torture. She shouldn't have yelled - she knew that and the regret of it had been sinking down on her.

"How long have you been with Xavier? I'm guessing not long since I've never seen you,"

"It's hard to explain," she said quietly, staring straight ahead. "In a way, three years." Cassie's eyebrows went up.

"How have I never seen you?"

A little smile flared on Izzy's lips.

"When I was here two years ago...Xavier kept me hidden. He didn't want anyone to even look at me. I left for a few years, but somehow I always end up in the same place," she chuckled, only then realizing she had been going on to a random stranger who she did not even know.

"Sorry, please don't mention any of this to him he's probably already-"

"Hey, it's okay. I won't," she set a hand on her shoulder, watching the obvious flinch but pushed it aside.

"Thank you," she let out a relieved sigh, continuing on their journey from store to store.

"Honestly, I don't see how you do it," Cassie sighed, looking over the shorter woman as she stared in the mirror, holding up a satin dress.

If Xavier gave her money, might as well put it to use before she's never allowed out again.

"What?" She turned to face Cassie, folding the dress over her arm.

"Be with him, be around him. He's...rude, arrogant. Dangerous. I can't imagine what it's like to actually be with him," Isabella's eyes zoned out for a moment, thinking of what she said. "Why even be with him if he's like that?"

"You say it like it's a choice," she sighed, looking over the other wracks of clothes.

She's heard the speeches, the questions, all of it was nothing new. Why be with him? Why stay? Just leave. It was never that easy. She had obviously tried before.

The first time...she shivered at the thought. That horrible, painful thought.

A thought for another day.

_____

Opening the door to their bedroom was like opening the door to the lion's den. Her nerves were on an all time high, anxiety through the roof as her and Cassie carried bags of clothes and other accessories in. Cassie glanced at her boss sitting on the edge of the bed, then to Isabella who didn't even dare look in his direction, just fumbling into the closet to begin putting things up.

After dropping off bags, Cassie left, leaving the two alone.

Upon hearing the door click, Isabella froze in fear within the closet, turning to Xavier who just stared at her, admiring her beauty.

"I..." she started, fidgeting with her fingers. "I'm sorry, I-I know I shouldn't have-"

"Give me a show," he cut her off, glancing at all the bags behind her, specifically the Victoria Secret bag.

She gulped, "What?"

"Give me a show of what you bought." He demanded, looking her dead in the eyes which she struggled to maintain.

She looked on at him, before lowering her head and nodding.

She walked back into the closet, slowly and hesitantly slipping her clothes off and he stared at her the whole time, watching more and more of her skin come to sight.

"That bag first," he pointed to the Victoria Secret bag causing her to blush a great deal but she still nodded.

She grabbed the first set her eyes laid upon - a white lace thong and matching bralette with little white flowers sewn into both.

Her footsteps were slowed as she nervously stepped out, grabbing at her arms roughly as she did so. His intimidating stare laid over her body, looking over the wonders of her curves.

He stood from the edge of the bed, approaching her but never saying a word. She didn't move, just watched his every move.

"I-I didn't mean to yell Xavier, I swear p-please just don't," she nearly burst out crying in anticipation.

He tsked, grazing his fingers over the lace of her bralette. "Your problem, Izzy, is you're so caught up in the bad things of our past," he slowly lowered to his knees, caressing along her thighs on the way down.

"To see that I would get on my knees and worship you, before I ever hurt you," he slipped his fingers in her thong, slowly moving it to the side, and taking a taste of her.

Upon the first moan that slipped from her parted lips, he yanked her closer, holding her ass and delving his tongue between her swelling folds.

Her hands dragged through his hair to keep herself from doubling over as his tongue laid flat on her clit and lapped at it.

He pleasured her more than she could handle, worshiping her, looking up at her with such lust for her.

Chapter 8

Her eyes batted open at the gentle rays of sunshine illuminating the room. It was well past eight in the morning, and as she rolled over Xavier was nowhere in sight, just the fresh scent of him lingering close by.

She plopped her hand down on his side of the bed, letting out a puff of air before her eyes searched the room.

"Xavier?" Her voice cracked some from just waking up.

She received nothing in return, leaving an uncomforting feeling to linger in her. Being alone was not her strong suit — especially having been punished for doing so, and forced to be around someone at all times.

She looked around the room again, going from the small conjoined rooms one by one. But in the end, it all turned up empty.

Her feet carried her slowly into the closet, feet sinking into the carpet at every step. Her nightgown dropped off her body, and she replaced it with a small dress — white with pink flowers embroidered into it. She covered her feet in cute little ankle socks, also having flowers on them to hide her feet from the cold wooden floor outside the room.

After doing her usual routine in the bathroom, She sucked in a deep breath while making her way down the hall, not knowing for sure if he was mad, even though experiencing the pleasures of last night. His moods were confusing.

She circled to his office, seeing it cracked, and slowly pushed it open to see what he was doing.

There he sat, hunched over his desk as he wrote speedily along some papers, but upon hearing the creak of the door his head snapped up.

His eyes wandered over her physique, wandering over her outfit and letting a small smile peek his lips—only the corner.

"Good morning," his voice gruffed out, fingers beckoning her towards him while he scooted his chair back.

"Good morning," she said in her usual soft tone, walking around the desk and climbing into his lap as he wished.

His first action was bringing her in for a kiss, not caring for her tense nature. She leaned into the kiss after a few seconds, hesitantly caressing his stubbled cheek.

The kiss was small, short, and simple.

"Nervous?"

She looked at him with a confused look. "Your first day is tomorrow," he answered and she nearly couldn't restrict her smile she tried to hide. She was afraid—what if he took it away if she was too excited? It could raise his suspicion of her. She couldn't risk anything.

Not with the tiniest glimpse of her freedom between the boulders of restriction.

"O-Oh, a little I guess," she shrugged, looking nervously at his features.

"Don't be, little red," he poked the tip of her nose and smiled, going down to her hips that straddled him and holding his hands there. "But also don't be stupid," he spoke slightly harshly, the shift in his tone startling her.

"There will be no talking to that boy," he grabbed her cheeks between his fingers painfully. "Or I will show you ten thousand times over what I'm capable of doing again." He stared at her with a cold look resting on his features, one that scared her to her very core and had her nodding her head in agreement.

"Good," he smiled lopsidedly, letting go of her cheeks and softly stroking them to soothe the pain that radiated through them.

She gulped and slowly lowered her eyes from his.

"Don't be like that baby, y'know I do this purely out of love for you," she wanted to scowl at him for saying that, but restrained herself greatly.

"H-How?" she dared to ask, not even being able to look at him.

"Because, Izzy," he tsked, running a hand through my hair, "You're beautiful. Every man that looks upon your beauty wants you. You're absolutely stunning, small enough for a man just to come and snatch you. I can't let that happen, now can I?" She slowly shook her head and leaned into him, putting her head in his neck as he held her as close as can be.

"No," she finally answered meekly.

―――――――――

He held her thigh softly as they rode down the road, getting closer and closer to the city. The ride so far had been silent, with nothing but the roaring engine and background music filling the air. Izzy kept her eyes out the window, slowly growing giddier—I was going to be alone without him, again. Getting away even just for a few hours was like the breath of fresh air she had been drowning to get to.

It was odd to her in a way. She hadn't been back for that long and he was already letting her do these things. Usually, she's not even allowed to come out of the room.

She turned her head to look at him, his eyes focused on the road but he could see her turn in the corner of his eye.

She stared at him for a moment—Has he really changed as he claims?

Well, not necessarily as he just threatened me earlier.

She let out a small huff and turned back, having the corner of Xavier's lips rise in a smirk as he wondered what she was thinking.

"I'm trusting you," He spoke, slightly startling her.

"What?"

"I'm trusting you with this. Last time I didn't trust you and it drove you away. I'm trusting you to be without me." They pulled into the little shop on the corner. He turned to her, looking her right in her green eyes and squeezing her thigh. "I can't lose you again. It broke me. I was too far gone without you." He nudged her head towards him and leaned in to kiss her softly. Her cheeks flourished in a soft blush and he smiled slightly at her.

He walked her out of the car and into the little café where the same two people stood behind the counter—Betty and Brandon. Betty welcomed the two with a warm smile, gesturing for Izzy to come her way but she hesitated.

Brandon eyed Xavier carefully, but when Xavier turned to him with a glare, he quickly turned away in no time. He had every right to be scared. After what happened last time.

"Hello dear! I'm so glad to see you again," Betty came out upon seeing Izzy not move and wrapped her arms around her in a warm hug. Isabella slowly wrapped her arms around her, smiling as she leaned into the hug.

"You too," The two smiled brightly at each other before Xavier came in and set a hand on the small of her back.

"I'll be back to get you at eight," she blushed as he nudged her head up and stole her lips, right in front of Brandon who looked away nervously.

"Antonio will stay here with you," her excitement died down in an instance as the hunk of a man walked through, an angry look

"But..."

"No buts, Izzy, be good."

———————————

Betty refreshed her on the basics of the job, watching Izzy as she handled a few customers and sharing her words of encouragement. There were times she would have awkward eye contact, but with the thoughts of Xavier's warning and Antonio's watchful eye. She did not doubt that Xavier told him of his hatred of Brandon.

Finally, it was nearing eight, also time for closing. Because of the lateness of the Year, night had already fallen, and she expected Xavier to be right on time. Currently, at 7:45, Antonio was in the bathroom, and Brandon was alone up front. She was nervous of course, but she needed to fix things—let him know she never wanted any of this to happen, for him to get involved.

"B..." She hesitated, but he heard and nearly went white seeing her.

"Get away from me before your guard dog sees you!" He snapped and went back to putting up trays with an angry look. She was heartbroken by his tone but pursued.

"Please just listen to me! W-We don't have much time I-"

"I don't care! I have nothing to say to you."

"I didn't want you to get involved, Brandon!" The two whisper-yelled back and forth, Izzy frantically looking back and forth down the bathroom hallway.

"All I tried to do is help you!" He raised his voice a bit and she panicked.

"I-I know that but I just—"

"And that's how I get paid back? I was in the hospital for weeks! And to see now you're just back with him!"

"C-calm down—"

"Calm down?! No! You need to hear this finally." he raged on and she was going to tell him to lower his voice when something stopped her.

A voice.

"Isabella."

Chapter 9

She fell with an oomph to the floor, panic flooding her body as she tried to scramble up, holding her head where he had pulled her hair.

"X-Xavier please!" She cried, backing against the wall as he yanked off his belt. At first she was afraid he'd strike her, but he threw it to the side.

"I think I've told you one too many times, Isabella." He raged in an unsettling calmness. "So maybe you need time to think on what you've done," before she could reach him to stop him, he was slamming the door shut and locking it from the other side where she couldn't go anywhere.

She begged, and whined and whimpered on the other half of that door for hours, begging him to listen to her and believe her. At a late hour he turned the power off, and the coldness of the night settled into their room and she swaddled herself in blankets as she cried the night away.

She feared the morning, or whenever he may come back.

2 years ago

"Xavier! Xavier please stop, PLEASE!" She panted, chasing after him as fast as she could as he dragged Brandon farther and farther down the stairs. She tried not to trip over her own two feet as she chased him down the stairs into the basement. Down the basement was a passageway that led further underground, where no one could hear him. No one could hear his cries, her begs and bargains to do anything if he just let him go.

Guards stood at the entrance of the passageway and Xavier gave them one glance and they stopped her, standing in front of her so she couldn't go any farther. She began to hyperventilate, trying to look over the buff men and looking around frantically.

Before finally she found the bright idea to slip under them and dart towards Xavier as he dragged a squirming and yelling Brandon away.

"Xavier please!" She cried, grabbing his arm and tugging as hard as she possibly could but he just continued to walk as if she hadn't even touched him.

Guards came to.stop her quickly, grabbing her by the arms but Xavier finally stopped, turning his head only slightly.

"Let her come. Keep her contained." He demanded with nothing more than a monotonous voice. The guards didn't relent on their grip on her arms, and led her behind the two even as she squirmed, but in the end she was just hurting herself.

Her heart pounded at a thousand miles per hour as they entered a dark room, locked by a large metal door. It was her first time being down here, it was dark and damp, filled by a strange smell she didn't even wish to know. But she did smell the faint scent of bleach mixed in. It scared her even more.

Xavier flipped on a light, the room being filled brightly but there was nothing in the room besides four concrete walls and a cabinet with multiple connecting shelves.

A struggling Brandon was thrown in the chair in the middle of the room and the guards let go of Isabella, going to help Xavier as she didn't know what else to do, didn't know how to help. They could kick her out of the room in an instant, with a flick of their fingers. They were too strong.

Their eyes met — hers and Brandon's — both frantic, both breathing heavy as he was strapped down. He didn't give up, didn't stop struggling against Xavier until he finally had enough and struck him with a fist to his cheek.

Brandon groaned while Isabella gasped and brought tears to her eyes, covering her mouth with both of her hands. Xavier glanced to her, seeing, feeling her emotion and it just made him more angry.

"So upset over a boy," he tsked, going around and grabbing him by the jaw as the guards went back to standing by her to make sure she didn't move.

He flipped out a knife and she began to freak out, guards grabbing her quickly as she just took a single step towards him. Xavier set the knife to his throat, watching him squirm but his eyes were on Isabella as she began to cry even more.

"What's so special abiut this boy, that you would cry for him?" Xavier questioned with a monotonous tone, looking down and inspecting Brandon who had gritted his teeth and tensed to the fullest.

"Maybe because I know how to treat her like a fucking human being— FUCK!" He gritted out and yelled as Xavier nicked his throat a little deep but not deep to puncture anything major.

"Xavier please..." Isabella continued to cry, and finally Xavier set the knife down on a little tray and sauntered towards her. He came up, cupping her cheeks and recieving a flinch in return.

"I'm doing this for you, little red, us, so no one can get in the way of what we have." He smiled against her cheek, laying a kiss on her cheek slowly and then pulling back.

He gave a gesture to his guards, and she was grabbed roughly with a hand over her mouth. She squealed and squirmed, bit down to try and get away from them but they were used to it all. It didn't phase them.

He grabbed the knife again, spinning it between his fingers before the next thing she saw, in a mere blink of an eye, it was dug into Brandon's shoulder.

He screamed bloody murder, squirming in the chair so much it nearly knocked himself over but Xavier's grip kept him from doing so.

Xavier rolled his eyes in annoyance, grabbed a rag and wrapping it roughly around his mouth to stop his annoying screams.

He glanced to Isabella as he tied a knot in that back of Brandon's head, seeing her eyebrows furrowed, his luscious locks of red curls now a frustrated mess, and tears pouring down her cheeks.

But Xavier ignored her this time. Doing what he thought needed to be done. For her. For them. Setting an example of what would be done if anyone tried to interfere in their relationship.

He took a crowbar that was locked away in the cabinet, setting it to the slid for the moment and grabbing a pair of black, leather gloves in one of the shelves.

He slipped them on leisurely, catching Brandon's eye whose were wide with fear and anxiety.

It made a smile crawl on his face, as in one quick movement he took the crowbar and whipped it across his face.

Brandon bit down so hard on the rag he thought his teeth were broken from the intense pain that overwhelmed his face.

Isabella let out a shrill scream and closed her eyes as she heard him land hit,

After hit,

After hit.

The screams Brandon let loose were agonizing, horrifying and it nearly made her want to get sick. The smell of blood leaked in the room as sometimes the end of the crow bar would get stuck on his skin, but Xavier would just merely rip it from him painfully.

Both Isabella and Brandon begged and screamed under the restraints of their mouths to stop, but Xavier didn't.

He moved the crow bar to his face, to his arms and hands, breaking each little finger of his and even the tendons in both hands.

He moved from their to his legs, where he broke one of his knees and then the other foot.

So there was no way to get away.

Chapter 10

The thoughts, the memories of what had happened with Brandon scared her to her core, and had her taking glances towards the double glass doors. She knew it was a bad idea, but wasn't it a worse idea to stay here? To be with him? He hadn't done anything bad to her besides lock her in their room, but she was still scared; scared he would snap at any moment and do something worse.

She creeped off the bed that she had been bundled in, her feet hitting the ground with pure hesitation.

But her mind made up quickly, and she was running towards the doors and opening them slowly to not make them creak. She looked back at her room, praying to God he didn't catch her, as she knew her life would be hell.

She creeped out onto the balcony, glancing around to see if any guards were near and the back behind her. There was no one, now was her time.

She climbed over the railing, holding onto it as she slid down it until the tips of her toes touched the rough material of the roof. Slowly and hesitantly she turned herself around, looking down to see she was still decently high up and a drop from this height could definitely hurt her. But she needed to be quick, Xavier could be back at any moment.

Her heart pounded in anticipation, slowly maneuvering down the slanted roof and her legs even wobbling slightly to scare her. Coming upon the edge she looked around for something soft to land on, or something she could step down on, but the only thing around were the pushes circling the house.

She gulped, knowing it was her only choice and sat down on the edge. Her eyes glanced all around once more, when the corner of her eye caught something.

A red blinking light. A camera, facing towards her.

Her eyes widened, and it was all it took for her to jump into the bushes and jump back up with adrenaline pumping in her veins. She took off towards the opening of woods, running as fast as she could because she knew she was already caught.

Xavier was watching.

He sat behind his desk, rolling his ring around his finger as his eyes watched her jump from the roof and dart for the woods. He shook his head, grinding his teeth as a certain anger filled him. He had tried. Over and over to be more lenient. But she just kept going against him purposely.

He gave her a nice home, better than what she had, he gave her love, wealth, endless pleasure.

Yet she still runs from him.

He opened his phone, going to his tracking app and watching as she ran through the woods. He had implanted a tracker on the necklace given to her, small, never to be noticed. In some way he could see this coming.

But she wouldn't get far. She would come back. She needs him, wants him. She would always come back to him.

She always has, and she always will.

_____

Sticks and little stones pierced into her feet the longer she ran, trickles of blood pouring down them. She was out of breath but scared to stop. Scared he was right on her tail. She couldn't stop, no matter how much her lungs begged her to.

She had made it out of the property, into an open field which had her even more scared. It was easy to spot her but thankfully the tall, dead grass covered most of her.

She ran and ran, spooking birds along the way and watching them fly up around her and into the sky.

But soon she couldn't run anymore, her legs gave out beneath her and she collapsed on the ground black dots filling her vision as she hyperventilated. I can't stop, she reminded herself, picking herself up weakly onto her hands and knees and slowly crawling.

Her fingers dug into the dirt, pushing herself forwards as she huffed and puffed for air, trying to gather herself to stand up.

— C'mon Izzy, c'mon.

She took a deep breath and pushed herself up, starting a slow jog and pushing herself to a run.

She ran through the fields, through the sidewalks of the highways with bustling cars honking at her and scaring her. She was afraid any one of them could be a familiar black car creeping up on her. Watching her.

Waiting to capture her.

He was close yet far, watching from a distance as he got things prepared.

He'd have everything prepared for her punishment.

Isabella made it to the city and that's when she finally stopped running. But it's also when regret began to sink in, the realization of her actions coming to light.

— Oh god…I ran. I fucking ran what the fuck was I thinking?!

Her nose tingles and burns with the feeling of wanting to cry as complete regret sunk into her being. She wanted to go back, she needed to go back but she was more than scared to. She didn't know what awaited her, what he would do to her.

Just the thought brought panic to her, but she was already in such a mess that she had caused either way it would be bad. Even if she had the slightest chance of getting completely away, he would somehow find a way to come back into her life. And it would be worse.

— "I'll lock you away and throw away the fucking key,"

She ran her hands harshly over her face and into her hair. His threat lived in her head, and before she knew it was was walking in the opposite direction.

Back through the city, through the highway and through the field. At this time it was late at night, her run had costed her hours away from home.

The night scared her, anything could happen without a trace left as she walked through the large field. Every little sound scared her, the sound of owls in the distance, bugs chirping away loudly close by.

She got into a light jog, but her tiredness was weighing her down tremendously.

She pushed herself, until she got through the opening of the woods and the manor stood high and mighty before her.

She gulped, twisting her fingers together but she was so close to passing out she didn't have a choice. Her legs hurt and ached, along with the rest of her body.

She got to the front door, no guards in sight to her surprise, and opening the door slowly.

Revealing Xavier who sat in his chair not far away, looking up as their eyes meet, when she fell to her knees and passed out.

Chapter 11

He tsked, picking her up off the floor and seeing the scratches and forming scabs, along with the dried blood on her legs and feet.

"Oh Izzy," he sighed, heading for the stairs except not going up them. He passed the set of stairs, going past them to a door with multiple locks which he had a guard unlock for him.

He descended down the set of stairs, the farther he went down, the darkness crept around the two until being consumed in complete darkness.

An automatic light flipped on and revealed another door on the other side of the room, also locked which the guard following unlocked for him. He stared down at his dear little red, watching the soft breaths that came from her parted lips. She looked absolutely exhausted.

It wouldn't compare to how she was about to be.

He walked leisurely down the hall full of cells, some even full of groaning occupants. The stench of bleach and blood was heavy, but he was used to it by now so it didn't phase him.

He walked for a while, coming across a special room built primarily for one purpose. One person. It wasn't like the others, empty with nothing but a chair.

This one had a mattress, with sheets lining it. It wasn't some old beat up mattress either. It looked rather new as well as the sheets. The room was clean, crystal clean. And there was a good light source.

It was better than any other cell, about as better as it could be.

He gently set her down on the mattress, looking down at her without a lick of emotion. Not even anger. Maybe just disappointed.

"You had done so good Izzy," he whispered with a tsk, pushing his hair out of his eyes and crouching down to stroke her cheek as she slept.

"But now you'll know the worst."

_____

She peeled her eyes open, her woozy vision making her dizzy as she tried to sit up. Her body felt heavy, tired and weak. Her arms were shaking just to hold herself up.

"I...I came back," she whispered weakly, looking up at Xavier who closed the door softly.

"Please, I came back," she nearly cried when looking around the room, recognizing it immediately from familiarity. "Please don't do this Xavier, I came back," she began to cry but he just watched with clenched fists.

"You still ran." Her eyes opened wide with tears, slowly shaking her head.

"X-Xavier...I came back. I came back for you...I-I love you please don't do this,"

"You love me?" She saw his eyes soften for a moment and nodded slowly, "You love me enough to run from me?" But in a moment they were gone and replaced with the hardness of his eyes that showed no emotion towards her.

"Maybe you'll finally learn your lesson down here," he turned to walk away, grabbing the handle of the door when she began to cry and beg, running towards him with the little strength she had left but the door was slammed in her face, and she fell back.

_____

Two years ago

He threw her into the empty cell, watching her fall with a thud and roll across the floor, even as she tried to get back up just as fast.

"Should've fucking known," he seethed, clenching his fists at his sides., all the whole shaking his head.

He walked over to her as she cowered away, grabbing her by the throat and shoving her against the wall where she screamed and began to cry.

"I-I'm sorry," she clawed at his hand as he began to squeeze harder with a look of nothing but pure anger.

"I've done nothing but love you Izzy," he said rather calmly, "NOTHING but give you all my love." He suddenly yelled and she flinched back, trying to cover her face and kick at his legs as her breath became faltered.

"I'm sorry," she wailed, but everything stopped.

When he put a gun to her head. She froze, her entire body tensing so hard it hurt.

"Do you even love me?" He asked calmly again, removing his hand from her throat which had her gasping for breath.

He pressed the gun against her forehead, digging it into her skin and stepping closer to her. Her mind was racing so much it had turned blank. She didn't know what to say, what to do.

Her boyfriend had a gun to her head. What was there to do?

"X-Xavier..." she breathed out with a hiccup. "I-I love you. I love you I promise," she cried.

"You ran," he snarled, flicking off the safety and she bags to cry harder.

"Please I won't ever again! Please Xavier please," she sobbed, holding her chest as if a way to stop her heart from pounding so hard in her chest. She couldn't feel her body, so scared everything had gone numb.

She slowly raised her hands with nothing more than hesitation as she cupped her hands around the one holding the gun.

"L-Listen to me," she pressed down on his hand, trying to get it to lower it when he finally did, away from her head and down to the ground. He watched her carefully, with nothing more than skeptical eyes.

"I love you. I made a-a mistake. Please, I love you," she cried, tear stains streaking her cheeks with swollen eyes and a pouty lip which wobbled.

"I love you," she repeated, over and over until he finally flicked the safety back on and put the gun back in his belt.

Her hand reached up and cupped his cheek, pulling him down to her level where she took his lips onto hers to prove her point farther. It was the first time she had chosen to kiss him, nothing was forced, just a small, sensual kiss filled with trembles. She couldn't get her body to stop shaking, the thought that he actually had a gun to her head, that he would have shot her would never leave her mind.

"You still ran," her eyes opened wide as he pulled back, and she thought he would pull his gun back out but he stood up and left out the door, and she heard the sound of multiple locks following with the jingle of keys.

She watched in silence, lips agape with nothing but shock.

He had locked her in here. In a tiny cell with nothing but a mattress and a few blankets. Not even a pillow.

He left her there. For two days to be exact. He had maids slip food and water through a little slit on the door. She had no human interaction for two days. Left with nothing but her thoughts. Her nightmarish thoughts filled with the fact her boyfriend almost shot her.

He had a gun…to my head, She thought.

She laid down on the mattress and cried. Cried for two days. Until he came back.

Chapter 12

It had been a week. No talking, no sound, barely any sight. She had no human interaction beside a maid sliding a plate of food under the flap.

But she barely ate. She felt too sick with herself to eat. She just sat in her little ball, knees to her chest and crying constantly.

She cried the entire week.

She never thought she would miss him so much, but she did in her own way.

She missed him with her entire heart, her entire being. His touch, his sweet words at times.

She had never missed something more in her life.

The need to be touched, to talk, to have someone to talk to was driving her insane.

She had witnessed no more than the creaky sound of the little flap opening every four hours. Other than that, complete and devastating silence. She had never hated quietness so much.

But what know, is Xavier was going insane as well.

A horrible, angry insanity that had him driving at an itch he couldn't scratch to touch the softness of her skin again.

He thrived on her touch, her comfort and her presence. Without her...

The two years of destruction for his enemies told enough.

He had gone long enough.

He headed down the stairs and into the hidden hallway guarded by his men.

Every step he got closer to that locked cell, his heart pumped a little harder. He was more than excited to see his love again, he couldn't stay angry at her. Not for long.

After all, she did come back.

He gestured tobhis guard before he even got up to her cell, and watched from afar as they quickly opened it.

And there she was.

Huddled in the likes of her sheets, squinted eyes as she blocked the rather bright light with her hand.

She looked sickly, paler than usual.

But he didn't care. He was just happy to see her.

He rushed into her cell, pulling the sheets gently from her body and carefully picking her up off the mattress.

She had little black spots filling her vision, which she had noticed started a few days ago. She had never passed out, but did feel the lightheaded effect of it. Mostly when she moved too fast.

But it seemed to be worse now.

To the point it was like time skips on the way upstairs. One second she was with him as he walked up the stares, and the next she was in the bathtub.

He watched her sluggish movements and her moments of black outs, holding her gently in his arms and whispering coos in her ear every time she'd wake.

"C'mon baby, let's get you in," he gruffed out when she opened her eyes in slits.

He held her in the tub as she was out like a light in a split second. An arm around her neck as he dunked her hair under.

He sighed. He had left her down there too long.

"Call Jerry," he yelled out to his guard waiting by the bathroom door. He heard the quick 'yes sir' and then footsteps decending away while he made the phone call.

After her bath he dried her off to the best of her ability and for the moment being, put a robe around her.

He stood her up with an arm around her waist and swiftly brushed her teeth and washed her mouth out.

After putting her under the covers, he got a warm rag and brought it to caress her face with it. "You're okay, little red," he muttered, stroking his index finger along her cheek.

Jerry came quick at the asking of his boss, having his med kit and a few other tools with him as he didn't know the problem.

But at seeing the sickly girl laying in bed, it was an easy guess.

He felt her pulse, and checked a few other things before making his diagnosis but it was pretty clear.

"She's extremely dehydrated, Xavier. I'll have to put her on an IV hopefully fir just a few hours and make sure she takes it slow. That should be good enough to nurse her back to health." Xavier nodded, looking back to his woman and kissing her knuckles as the doctor began to find a good vein to put an IV in.

It took a few hours, late into the night when she began to open her eyes more than slowly.

She looked around, spotting the fluid going into her arm and the large man sleeping soundly beside her, his hand captured around hers. He was in pajama pants and no shirt, his heat radiating onto her arm.

She noticed the robe she was in which was rather uncomfortable to sleep in, no matter the soft feeling of satin on her skin.

She slowly got up, taking her IV set up with her as she stepped into the closet and shut the door to block the light from waking him up.

She picked out a tank top and pajama pants as well but when she tried to take her shirt off her IV dug in her the wrong way and made her grimace.

She struggled to get her shirt off, nearly crying in frustration when she heard a yell from the other room.

"Isabella? Isabella?!" Xavier yelled in panic and near anger. It scared her, she had never heard so much panic from him it made her quickly open the door with her shirt over her naked breasts.

Xavier was sat up straight, clenching the sheets as he breathed heavy. His heart was pounding in his chest she could've almost heard it from across the room.

He rushed over to her, wrapping his arms around her and she felt his heart beating in his chest at a heavy rate.

"I-I'm here," she stuttered as he squeezed her harder, her shirt dropping to the floor where her breasts pushed against his naked chest.

"I thought you left me again," he breathed into her neck with a sigh, pulling back and looking iver her, eyes darkening at the look of her.

"I-I struggled with my shirt because of my—"

"You can take it out now, it's been about four hours." He lifted her arm and gently took the IV out but waited to take the other piece out before getting bandage wrapping.

When getting it, he gently pulled the small piece out gently and wrapped her arm. He knew he should've waited for the doctor but wanted her to be comfortable.

"Let's go to bed." He looked over the sweet swells of her breasts, tugging her arm towards the king sized bed but she looked back into the closet.

"But...my shirt," she spoke meekly, blushing as he laid her on the bed and nearly covered herself.

"You won't need one."

Chapter 13

He sets himself over top of her, towering over her and feeling her little heart beat faster underneath him. Thumping up and onto his chest.

The feeling of his skin on her again had her turned on almost immediately, the softness, the inked skin touching and rubbing against her had her legs raising around his waist and wrapping around as best as she could.

Her arms came up and wrapped around his neck as he kissed down her chest to have her arching her back. He reached her stomach, feeling her shiver beneath him as he lowered her pajama pants slowly. No underwear was found underneath, just the very thin, light stubble of her core. She hadn't shaven in the past week for obvious reasons, but he didn't care.

His tongue dipped into her slit, feeling her hips raise off the bed and into his mouth while he worked on getting her pants off to leave her bare in front of him.

He looked up at her as he ate her, feasted upon her like the predator he came off to be. He clawed at her hips, tugging lightly on her skin while she dug her hands in his hair. She felt the soft, strands of his dark brown hair, nearly black but had a red toning to give it off as brown.

She moaned, "Xavier..." squeezing her thighs around his head.

"I'm here, baby," he said deeply, going back to eating her and taking a hand of hers in his. Their fingers interlocked with each other, savoring each other and soon enough he was pounding her deeply into the bed.

Her face buried in the pillow as he thrust from behind, hearing moan after moan and feeling her stomach clench around him.

He was leaned over her, a hand over her lower stomach and pushing lightly just to have her moan a little louder.

His eyes followed the curve of her waist — she looked skinner than when he first brought her back.

He then followed the curve of her ass, biting his lip and thrusting in harder and fighting the urge to slap her plump ass. He didn't wish to be rough with her.

He slowed his thrusts upon hearing her cries, going slowly and circling his hips to hit her perfect spot. He watched as she clenched the pillow cases in her hands and bit down on the pillow with her eyes squeezed closed.

"Fuck...Dammit Izzy," he didn't last his usual ten to twenty minutes, instead only lasting about seven from not seeing her, feeling her, tasting her.

"X-Xavier," she moaned his name and led a smile to play on his lips. He licked over his canines and sped back up.

She was his drug, and he was a fiene.

The morning was dreadful, full of Grey skies spilling their tears into the earth.

She felt it as she woke up, scared as she saw the bed empty and made, not a light on in the bathroom.

She felt the same fear he felt a night before.

"Xavier?!" She screamed. Oh no, no no, he locked me away again. He locked me away!

She sprinted to the door, getting ready to yank it when the door busted open and Xavier rushed in, nearly running over her.

"Izzy, are you okay?" He asked in a panic, cupping her cheeks and kneeling down as she sunk into the floor, a crying mess.

"Please don't lock me away again!" She cried, head down and tugging on his shirt. "Please I'll do anything Xavier please!" He blinked a few times, hesitantly bringing her to hug him.

"Shh," he soothed, "You're with me, little red," he whispered.

She gripped onto him so tightly it had his lips parting in surprise.

He had done too much this time.

Almost worse than after he had a gun to her head.

She hadn't slept for weeks when that happened, and stayed ten feet away from him at all times.

He petted her ginger curls, whispering sweet nothings in her ear till she finally calmed down.

"Our friends are coming over tonight, baby," he changed the subject to try and make her feel better.

"W-Who?" She sniffled, refusing to let go of him.

"Jason and Sam. You like Sam, remember?" She nodded, wiping her eyes with one hand.

"They'll be coming around six," he whispered, kissing her forehead.

"Why don't we get you some food? Are you hungry?" She shook her head and he frowned.

"Isabella, you are not skipping meals," he stood up and took her with him, holding her around her waist and bringing her down stairs where plates of food were being served by his cooks.

He led her by hand and sat her in one of the chairs, pushing her in and then taking his seat beside her. He began to pile food onto her plate but she just looked at it all with distaste. She took her fork slowly, picking at her food with a few nibbles here and there.

"Izzy, please eat," he wrapped his arm over her shoulders, picking up her fork and stabbing a piece of egg then holding it to her lips.

"I'm not hungry," she shook her head away from the food with furrowed brows. She pushed his arm away with her wrist, getting the food away from her face.

He sighed, putting the fork back.

"You need to eat, Isabella." He stated a little more harshly, getting frustrated at her lack of nutrition. He didn't need her passing out on him.

"Just a few bites, c'mon baby," he forcibly smiled, picking up the fork once more and watching her hesitate before opening her lips.

He sighed and smiled, watching her chew and then take only a few more bites but it was better than nothing. As long as she had at least something on her stomach.

———————

As the evening came, Isabella sat up in their room as she proceeded to get ready, all the while Xavier stayed downstairs — even though not wanting to. But his guests were here and he didn't want them to feel uncomfortable.

"Where's Isabella? I haven't seen her in so long," Sam asked with a crooked smile. She had never liked him, Xavier never cared in all honesty. She was a friend to his love, that's all that mattered. She knew she needed at least somebody. Or she would definitely go insane. No matter if they liked him or not.

It's just if they acted on their disliking.

Xavier glanced up the stairs to the light on under the shut door of their bedroom.

"Getting ready. She should be down soon." Sam nodded and quickly went back to her husband who looked around the mansion at the different pieces of hanging art.

"I'll go check on her," the two nodded as Xavier headed up the stairs and to their bedroom where he pushed the door open slowly to peek in.

"Izzy?" He asked softly, seeing her on the bed staring blankly into the mirror.

He shut the door softly behind him, going to her and kneeling down in front of her. He tucked a curl behind her ear, looking over her with a certain worry he felt deep in his chest.

"Sam is asking for you, do you want to go downstairs?" She turned her head down to look at him and slowly nodded, taking his hand of which he held out for her and letting him lead her out the door and down the stairs where their friends awaited. Upon seeing Isabella, a huge grin spread over Sam's lips but faltered upon her blank and empty stare. Either way, she rushed to her and wrapped her arms around her while the two men began to chat about their partners, watching their interactions, Jason with a smile on his face while Xavier held an unemotional one, watching Izzy closely and studying her interaction as Sam talked her ear off.

He would watch as she gulped and glanced towards him each time before responding. It made his eyes squint at her.

"How have you been? I haven't seen you in forever. What...what happened?" Sam asked worriedly, also taking a cautious glance towards Xavier and even taking the step to move her more away from him when asking.

"What do you mean?" Izzy simply asked, folding her hands in front of her when Sam finally let them go.

"Well..." again she glanced towards Xavier who luckily didn't catch her glance, too busy in a conversation with Jason.

"Last time we talked, you...you were a mess. You were begging me to run with you, and then you went missing for two years?" Sam blinked multiple times, looking over Izzy and seeing the necklace around her neck, more elegant than Jason had ever given her and definitely more expensive. She then glanced at the dress she wore, a light brow tied in the front and rather stunning on her. But she looked so frail, so skinny.

"I...I'd rather not talk about it. Come, I'm sure dinner is almost ready," Izzy has very a forced smile, gesturing towards the table.

"We can run, Isabella. I'll go too. Anything to get you away from this...this man," she said the last word with pure disgust, but tugged along her arm as if to get her to go now.

"I don't need to run Sam, I-I'm happy so let's just—"

"Happy? With a man who abuses you?"

"He doesn't a-abuse me, please let's sit—" she tried again to gesture towards the table but Sam cut her off once more.

"You're underweight Izzy he's obviously starving you too!"

"STOP!" She suddenly yelled, making all three turn to her with such a shocking look marking their features. Even Xavier, shocked to hear her yell out of nowhere.

He came to her side, seeing the tears that brimmed her eyes. He took her arm gently, rubbing her back and then casting his eyes along the two.

"I think it's best if both of you left, now."

Printed in the USA
CPSIA information can be obtained
at www.ICGtesting.com
LVHW021205081123
763364LV00067B/1170